The Mystery of Socks

By Pam Hazlehurst

AuthorHouse™ UK Ltd.
1663 Liberty Drive
Bloomington, IN 47403 USA
www.authorhouse.co.uk
Phone: 0800.197.4150

© 2014 Pam Hazlehurst. All rights reserved.

No part of this book may be reproduced, stored in a retrieval system,
or transmitted by any means without the written permission of the author.

Published by AuthorHouse 03/19/2014

ISBN: 978-1-4918-9702-7 (sc)
978-1-4918-9703-4 (e)

Any people depicted in stock imagery provided by Thinkstock are models,
and such images are being used for illustrative purposes only.
Certain stock imagery © Thinkstock.

This book is printed on acid-free paper.

Because of the dynamic nature of the Internet, any web addresses or links contained in this book may have changed since publication and may no longer be valid. The views expressed in this work are solely those of the author and do not necessarily reflect the views of the publisher, and the publisher hereby disclaims any responsibility for them.

Thank you to my husband for his constant support and also my best friend Carole.

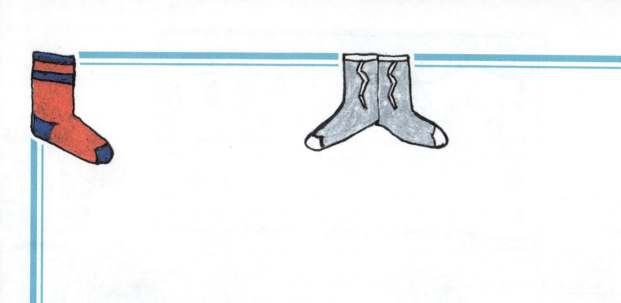

How many times do we hear our mums say.

Whatever happens to socks on a washday?

Into the washing machine in pairs they go.

But when they come out some are odd.

Why is that so?

Mum says, socks must sprout feet.

And that has to be true!

Cos my mum doesn't lie!

So I believe that too!

At the back of the machine I bet
there's a little trap door.

Where those odd socks squeeze
through to escape I'm sure.

I wonder where they go when they run free?

If anyone knows, would you
please tell mum and me?

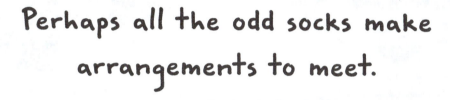

Perhaps all the odd socks make arrangements to meet.

Then all catch a bus at the end of the street!

A day trip to the countryside,

or even the lakes.

I do hope they remember to take sandwiches and cakes!!

They might ride in a rocket and zoom up to the stars.

Or go for a visit on planet Mars!

Is it possible, aliens have the same problems we do?

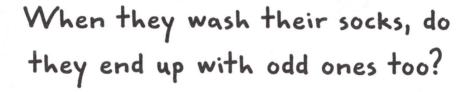

When they wash their socks, do they end up with odd ones too?

What if they go to London and call on the queen for the day.

Go inside Buckingham Palace.

Wow!! Wouldn't that be ok.

Be served with hot buttered crumpets

And jam and cream scones.

Then later play with her corgis,

until it was time to go back home.

I think, they might fly on an aeroplane
to somewhere hot and sunny.

Imagine that! Socks wearing sun hats.

Wouldn't that look funny!

Go to the beach with buckets and spades.

Go for a swim in the sea.

Then at the end of a perfect day
have burger and chips for tea!

So next time on a washday, when you're puzzled and thinking it's you.

Cos you have found some socks are missing.

Please mum's don't be blue!

Those socks must have found that trapdoor and decided to go on the run.

And will probably be out there, having lots of fun!!

Lightning Source UK Ltd.
Milton Keynes UK
UKOW06f1433140514

231594UK00008B/32/P